Sara Rose,
Kid Lawyer

"For every kid who loved to argue and was told they would make a great lawyer."

By Spencer M. Aronfeld

Illustrated by Floyd Yamyamin

AuthorHouse™
1663 Liberty Drive
Bloomington, IN 47403
www.authorhouse.com
Phone: 1-800-839-8640

First published by AuthorHouse 11/11/2010

ISBN: 978-1-4520-7515-0 (sc)

Library of Congress Control Number:
2010912050

...free paper.

author**HOUSE**®

Sara Rose was only ten years old, but she sure liked to argue. She argued with her parents about what time to go to sleep. She argued with her grandmother about what to do on the weekends. She argued with her friends about what clothes to wear. She argued with her teachers about doing homework.

But her all-time favorite person to argue with was her little brother, Nory. Sara Rose argued with Nory about everything. She argued about who would sit in the front seat of the car, who would eat the first slice of pizza, and who got to control the television's remote.

Most of the time, Sara Rose won her arguments.

One day in class, she was arguing with her teacher, Mrs. Baldwin, about not going to PE, when her teacher said something very strange.

"Sara Rose," Mrs. Baldwin said, "since you like to argue so much, you should be a lawyer." This took Sara Rose by surprise. She didn't know what a lawyer was. But if it meant she would get to argue and Mrs. Baldwin thought it was something Sara Rose was good at, it sounded like fun.

"Okay, Mrs. Baldwin, I am a lawyer."

"Oh no, Sara Rose, kids can't be lawyers; it's something that you have to become when you grow up."

"Well, why can't I be a lawyer right now?"

"Sara Rose, I am not going to argue with you about that too. Now go to PE."

For Sara Rose, growing up would take too long; she wanted to be a lawyer right away.

Across the street from Sara Rose's house, her friend Ellie always set up a lemonade stand on the weekends. She had a big sign, painted with mostly bright red letters, that said *Ellie and Isaac's Homemade Lemonade—5 Cents*. The word *Lemonade* was painted bright yellow.

Ellie and her little brother, Isaac, would sit there all day with a pitcher of ice water, sliced lemons, and packages of sugar. Isaac would squeeze the lemons; Ellie would add the sugar and stir it up to make lemonade. They had a stack of small Dixie cups that Isaac would take from the bathroom sink. Any time a car would pass by, which was not often, they would yelp and scream and try to get the driver to stop and buy lemonade.

On a good day, they would sell five or six glasses of lemonade and drink the rest themselves.

One Saturday, Sara Rose decided to open up her own stand. But instead of selling lemonade, she put up a sign saying *Sara Rose's Arguments—5 Cents*. She had painted the words on the back of her Jonas Brothers poster and then taped it to the side of a cardboard box she had found in the garage. She had not been sure how to spell *argument*, so she had looked it up in the dictionary.

She took an old fish bowl and taped to it a little piece of paper that said *5 Cents* so that it would be like a cash register for her customers. She went ahead and put a few nickels in there so that Ellie and Isaac would see that she had already made some money.

Sara Rose took two folding chairs that her mom saved for her card games. She put one chair in front of the box, with a small sign saying *Customers*, and one behind the box, with another small sign that said *Sara Rose*. Finally, she sat down, crossed her arms, and smiled. She put the dictionary under her chair just in case, along with her notebook and some colored markers.

Not one car stopped for Sara Rose's argument stand. She sat there all morning and watched people drive by. There were a few people who stopped across the street to buy Ellie's lemonade, however. They sipped their lemonade and stared at Sara's stand, but nobody walked over.

After several hours, a man driving a blue convertible stopped to buy lemonade. With his paper cup in hand, he walked across the street to Sara's stand. He had a grey beard and little, round glasses. He was wearing a blue shirt with buttons on the collar so that the collar would not fly away.

"Good morning, sir," Sara Rose said. "Would you like to buy an argument?"

"Why are you selling arguments?" he asked.

"Well, sir, my name is Sara Rose and I love to argue. My teacher, Mrs. Baldwin, told me that I'm so good at it that I should become a lawyer when I grow up. But I want to see if I can make it a business now, like Ellie with her lemonade."

"Well, that's wonderful," the man replied. "My name is Harold and I'm a lawyer. But you know, lawyers don't just argue for the sake of arguing. In fact, Sara Rose, most lawyers don't argue at all. And when we do argue, it's to help people who can't argue for themselves."

"What? I thought lawyers got to argue all the time," she said.

Harold smiled and took another sip of lemonade. "May I have a seat?" he said, pointing to the empty chair.

Sara noticed Ellie and Isaac staring at her and Harold from across the street. She smiled and said, "Sure. You're my first customer."

"You see," he said, taking a seat, "lawyers who argue the most are called litigators. And they don't argue for themselves but for other people, their clients. Clients are what lawyers call their customers. And when they help their customers—or clients—they are representing them."

Sara took out a piece of paper and started to write down some things: *lawyer's customers=clients*.

"And when a lawyer works, they call it practicing," he explained.

"You mean, like I have to with my piano on the weekends?" Sara Rose asked.

"Sort of, but lawyers call their work practicing even though they do it as a job. And it's not just on weekends but every day.

Oh, Sara thought, *this is more complicated than I imagined.* She wrote down: *lawyer's work = practicing. Every day.*

Harold continued to explain, "When lawyers help their clients, they call it representing clients. That's what lawyers do—they represent people or things."

Sara wrote: *lawyer's help = represent.*

"Some lawyers help their clients buy and sell things. Those lawyers are called transactional lawyers." Sara Rose did not write that down, because she did not know how to spell *transactional.*

"Some lawyers help their clients with tax problems; they're called tax lawyers. Some help people who have to file bankruptcy, and they're called bankruptcy lawyers." She did not write that down either.

"Others work for the government, the police, hospitals, schools, husbands and wives getting divorced, or people adopting children. There are many different kinds of lawyers, just like there are many different kinds of doctors."

"And what are the lawyers called again who get to argue all the time?" Sara Rose said. "I forgot."

"Litigators," Harold said, smiling. "Or trial lawyers."

Sara Rose wrote down *Trial Lawyers* and drew a red circle around it.

"How did you become a lawyer?" Sara Rose asked.

"Well, I had to go to a special school called law school. I did that after I graduated from college. College usually takes four years, and then law school takes another three years."

Harold went on to explain, "And only those people who get good grades in school get to go to college and law school. It starts with getting good grades in grammar school.

"And even if you get good grades, you still have to take a special test to go to law school. It's called the LSAT, or the Law School Admissions Test."

Sara did some adding in her head and then said, "You mean it takes seven years of school and then I could become a lawyer too?"

"Not yet, Sara Rose. All law students, once they graduate from law school, have to take more tests to make sure they understand the law of the particular state they want to practice in.

"You see, each state has different and complicated laws that change almost every day, and the lawyer has to know the laws in order to become a lawyer.

"You have to take a test called the bar exam. The bar is the railing that separates lawyers from the audience in a courtroom. So the bar exam is the test that separates lawyers from non-lawyers.

"Each state also has very strict rules about who can become or stay being a lawyer. People who have done bad things or have been in trouble with the law usually can't become lawyers.

"And even once you become a lawyer, you have to continue to take classes and study for the rest of your life by going to seminars and reading.

"When you finally become a lawyer, you get a special permission to practice law. And you have to take an oath promising to be a good lawyer.

"Finally, you would get a law license."

"You mean like a driver's license?" Sara Rose asked.

"Yes, you have to follow the rules, or you could lose the license. If lawyers break the law, lie, steal, or cheat, they lose their license. You see, Sara Rose, it's an honor to be a lawyer.

"There are many great lawyers. Do you know any famous ones?" he asked.

"No," Sara Rose said.

"Here are a few that might surprise you: President Abraham Lincoln was a lawyer; Mahatma Gandhi was a lawyer; President Obama is a lawyer; Clarence Darrow and Gerry Spence are considered to be the best trial lawyers;* Secretary of State Hillary Clinton is a lawyer; and First Lady Michelle Obama is a lawyer.

"You see," he continued, "none of those lawyers like to argue just to argue. They argue in order to help people. Being a real lawyer means more than just being able to argue. It means that you can argue to make a positive difference in somebody's life.

"Then, when you win an argument, hopefully you have made things better than they were before. That's what lawyers call justice."

Harold looked at his watch and then stood up to shake Sara Rose's hand.

"Thank you, sir," she said.

Harold reached into his back pocket, pulled out his wallet, and took out a little white card. In small, black letters, it said *Harold Stanley, Attorney at Law.*

---

* Both have been inducted in the Trial Lawyer Hall of Fame.

That night, sitting in her bed, Sara Rose carefully outlined Harold Stanley's card on pieces of pink construction paper. After cutting several pieces to the same size, she took out a marker and wrote: *Sara Rose, Kid Lawyer*.

The next morning, Sara Rose, for the first time in her life, got to school early. She was relieved to find that her classroom door was unlocked. Before anyone else arrived, she put one of her new cards in each of her classmates' desks. She also put one in her teacher's desk.

After the bell rang, Mrs. Baldwin opened her desk to find the small, pink card. She held it in her hand and looked directly at Sara Rose.

"Sara Rose, please come to my desk. What is this all about?"

Sara Rose explained her meeting with Mr. Stanley and how she now understood that great lawyers do not argue just to argue, but rather to help people or things that cannot argue for themselves, and that those people or things are called clients. Mrs. Baldwin smiled and put the card in her wallet to show the other teachers during the lunch hour.

Each morning after the Pledge of Allegiance, the principal made an announcement over the school's loudspeaker.

On this particular day, the principal, Mrs. Avery, said she had some news for the students.

In a squeaky voice, she announced: "Due to cuts in the budget for operating the school, there is no funding for the computers we wanted for the fourth-grade classroom."

The class groaned; they had been promised they would get computers in the classroom this year. Even Mrs. Baldwin had a sad look on her face, and she couldn't help but notice that in the middle of all the frowns, Sara Rose sat there with a big smile like it was Christmas morning.

"What are you so happy about, Ms. Sara?" the teacher said. "Didn't you just hear that we're not going to get our computers?"

"I'm happy," Sara Rose said, "because I just got my first client." She stood up, looked at her classmates, and said, "I'm going to argue for us, as to why we have to have computers in our classroom."

Everybody laughed, and Sara Rose turned a little red.

"Wait a second," Mrs. Baldwin said to the students. "Hold on, be quiet, children." The class settled down.

Sara Rose said to Mrs. Baldwin, "I'm not kidding. I want to go see Mrs. Avery so I can argue that we should have computers.

"But first, I need to get ready, and I need your help," she said, addressing her classmates.

Mrs. Baldwin said, "I'm listening." In fact, they were all listening.

Sara said, "Mrs. Baldwin, can I write something on the chalkboard?"

Mrs. Baldwin said she could, and Sara Rose grabbed some chalk and handed it to Andy, a boy who was always telling his friends about the cool things he did at home on his computer.

"Okay," Sara Rose said to Andy, "now make a list from one to twenty on the chalkboard."

"But there are thirty-two of us in this class," said Mrs. Baldwin.

"Okay, Andy, please make a list from one to thirty-two, accounting for each student in the class," Sara Rose said.

As Andy began listing the numbers, Sara Rose said, "Now listen, everyone, I need you to tell me one thing you need a computer for—something you can't do without one. It doesn't matter if it's big or small, smart or dumb. Just give me an idea."

"Class, this is called brainstorming," Mrs. Baldwin said. "That's when a group uses its ideas and energy to come up with things we would not be able to come up with by ourselves."

"Yeah, whatever," Sara Rose replied. "I just need someone to start calling things out."

"I got one, Sara Rose!" Peter Garcia jumped up and raised his hand.

"Yes, Peter?" Sara answered, sounding a little like Mrs. Baldwin.

"We need computers to go to Club Penguin, my favorite Web site." Everybody laughed.

"Hey, hey," Sara reminded the class, "there are no bad ideas here. Andy, please write that down."

"How do you spell *penguin*?" he asked. Everyone laughed again.

"I don't know," said Gretchen, "but if I had Google, I could find out. Wait ... that's another one! Andy, write that down."

Then Billy raised his hand. "I like to use the computer to see what the weather is and if I need to bring a sweater to school."

"Good one," Sara Rose said.

Millie said, "My parents use the computer to send e-mails to my grandparents. I would like to learn how to do that too."

Burt said, "I like to go on Skype so I can talk to my brother who's stationed in Iraq."

"Where's Iraq?" Juan said.

"See!" Gretchen responded. "If we had Google, I could show you and then even tell Billy what the weather is like there today." Billy liked that.

Jennie said, "I like to do my research for school projects." Mrs. Baldwin seemed to like that answer.

Clifton said he used it to practice chess on days that there was no chess club after school.

Zach used the computer to Photoshop his campaign posters for the school election.

Bernice wrote her poetry on the computer. And the list went on.

Finally, after about an hour, the class stared proudly at the thirty-two ideas neatly written on the chalkboard. Some were good; some were great. All of them were things that could be done better and faster with a computer. Some of them could not be done at all without a computer.

Sara Rose quickly wrote the list down in her notebook and asked Mrs. Baldwin if she could go see Mrs. Avery now. Mrs. Baldwin promised to see what she could do about getting Sara Rose an appointment but said that the entire class had math work to do now.

The next day, when class started, Mrs. Baldwin called Sara Rose to her desk.

"Sara Rose, Principal Avery has agreed to see you about the computers. But I want you to know that her mind is pretty well made up. I don't want you to be upset if you can't change her mind."

Sara Rose grabbed her notebook and quickly walked to the principal's office. The only other time she had ever been to Mrs. Avery's office was when she was in trouble. She gripped the notebook tightly in her hands; her palms were sweaty.

"The principal will see you now, Sara Rose," the secretary said.

Sara Rose walked slowly into the principal's office knowing she had to summon all of her experience in arguing to win this case for her class.

"Yes," Principal Avery said, not even looking up from the big stack of paper on her desk.

"Ma'am," Sara Rose said quietly. Her voice wasn't sounding quite right to her. "I am here to represent my fourth-grade class." She handed Mrs. Avery one of her pink cards.

"What?" the principal said. "I can't hear you."

"I am here because of my class," she repeated, this time maybe a little too loud. "We need computers in our classroom."

"Oh yes, Mrs. Baldwin told me you would be stopping by this morning. I'm sorry, Sara Rose, but there were budget cuts and there are problems with paying for certain things. If I could make it happen, we would have computers. We just can't afford them. Period. So please go back to your classroom now. I'm very busy. Sorry."

Sara stood there with her card still in her extended hand. Mrs. Avery had not yet looked up. So she placed the card down on top of the stack of papers.

Mrs. Avery picked it up, moved her glasses down her nose, read the card, and smiled.

"But I have this list of reasons I prepared with my class," Sara said.

"Sara, look, I'm very busy, and you need to return to your class now."

"Ma'am," Sara Rose said, "I need to just tell you something very quickly. Can I, please? Please?" Sara said using her special, last-ditch effort voice she saved for special occasions.

"Okay," Mrs. Avery said, relenting.

"I have a list of thirty-two reasons why we need to have computers in our classroom. Can I read them to you?"

"I really don't have time. Just leave them here on my pile of papers, and I'll get to them this week. I promise. Now, get back to class, Sara Rose."

Sara Rose left the list on the principal's desk and then walked slowly back to class with her head down. She thought about what she was going to say to Mrs. Baldwin and her classmates. You see, Sara Rose was not used to losing arguments.

When she got to her classroom, she quietly took a seat and quietly told them what happened. Mrs. Baldwin told everyone to get back to their studies.

That night, Sara Rose went to sleep and tried to forget about it all.

The next day, when school started, Mrs. Baldwin called Sara Rose to her desk.

"Sara Rose, the principal spoke to me this morning and asked me to ask you to go with her to speak to the school board next week to make your argument about the computers."

Sara Rose didn't know what that meant, but the smile on Mrs. Baldwin's face seemed to suggest it was a good thing. She gave Sara Rose a green permission slip to take home to her parents to sign.

That weekend, Sara Rose was having lemonade at Ellie and Isaac's stand when Mr. Stanley drove up in his blue convertible. Sara said hello, gave him one of her cards, and told him about her first case.

Mr. Stanley explained that what Sara Rose was doing was something called an appeal.

"Even when a lawyer loses an argument, or a trial, they can take their argument to the next level or a higher court." In this case, Sara Rose did not win the argument with Mrs. Avery, but she still had a chance to win the case for her class with the school board.

That next Monday, Mrs. Avery was waiting for Sara Rose when she arrived to class. She drove Sara Rose to a big brown building downtown. There was a large room that looked like a movie theatre, with many people sitting on the stage. There were bright lights and a microphone, and in front of the stage, there was a little stepstool.

Mrs. Avery got up and introduced Sara Rose to the audience as a member of her school's fourth-grade class. She said that Sara Rose was there to explain why her class needed to have computers.

Sara Rose stepped on to the little stool. She looked directly at the people and felt her legs shaking. Mrs. Avery handed Sara Rose the list Sara had left on her desk.

Sara Rose spoke into the microphone, and suddenly her voice sounded very important. "My name is Sara Rose. I am ten years old, a fourth grader, and I represent my classmates. We need to have computers, and I have thirty-two reasons why."

The school board members listened closely to her. One even seemed to be taking notes.

After Sara was done, they decided to hold a vote on whether to reconsider having computers in the classroom.

There were fourteen people on the stage, and ten raised their hands, agreeing that her class did, in fact, need computers.

Sara Rose had won her first case!

She went back to school and reported the good news to her class. Everyone cheered, and Mrs. Baldwin gave Sara Rose a hug.

A week later, thirty-two boxes were delivered to Mrs. Baldwin's class. Every fourth grader had a computer thanks to a little fourth-grade girl who liked to argue.

Look out for two new books from Spencer Aronfeld.

kid Lawyers to the Rescue

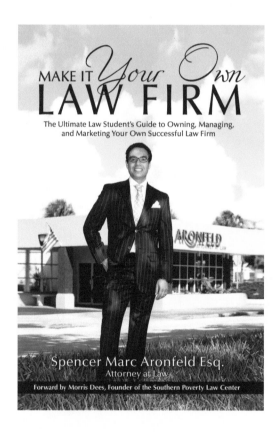

About the Author

Spencer Aronfeld has enjoyed powerful courtroom victories over Walt Disney World, Wild Oats, P.A.C. Construction, Fedan Tire, and Todel Apartments and has gained international recognition as a lawyer for the people.

Born in Chicago, Illinois and raised in Wichita, Kansas, Aronfeld graduated *cum laude* from the University Of Miami School Of Law in 1991. Upon graduation, he founded his own firm, in Coral Gables, Florida. He has dedicated his life to representing individuals against corporate giants, such as the Florida Marlins, Bayside Marketplace, Jackson Memorial Hospital, Miami Dade County, Mt. Sinai Hospital, Royal Caribbean Cruises, LTD., State Farm Insurance Company, United Automobile Insurance Company, and International Airplane Leasing.

Aronfeld earned international recognition after his first jury trial, when an Orlando, Florida jury awarded his Uruguayan clients a $100,000.00 verdict against Walt Disney World. Before trial, Disney had offered his clients only $1,200.00. That verdict remains one of the largest in a personal injury case against the Mouse and his legal battle was recounted in the book, *Disney, the Mouse Betrayed*. The story is currently in preproduction with a major Hollywood studio.

Aronfeld graduated from the Trial Lawyer College, a non-profit institution founded and directed by legendary trial lawyer, Gerry Spence in Dubois, Wyoming. Lawyers are admitted by invitation only and learn how to try cases on behalf of the people. Aronfeld has since returned as part of the faculty and has joined Spence on several of his nationwide book tours.

Aronfeld has hosted his own weekly radio talk show and lectures frequently around the country. He has appeared on the *Today Show, Court TV, Primer Impacto, Montel, Dateline NBC, America's Most Wanted, The Insider* and *CNN*.

Aronfeld is a Board Certified Civil Trial Lawyer by both the Florida Bar and the National Board of Trial Advocacy. He is AV rated by Martindale Hubbell.

Once again in 2009 he was recognized as one of *Florida's Super Lawyers* and South Florida Legal guide named him among the Top Lawyers in South Florida.

In addition to the Florida Bar, he is admitted to practice in Federal Court, the District of Colombia and the United States Supreme Court.

He is a member of American Justice Association, Miami-Dade Justice Association, Trial Lawyers for Public Justice and an Eagle Member of the Florida Justice Association.

Sara Rose, Kid Lawyer is his first published book. A portion of the proceeds of this book go to Lawyers to the Rescue, a not for profit corporation.

www.lawyerstotherescue.org

ARONFELD

TRIAL LAWYERS

Spencer Aronfeld, Esq.

3132 Ponce de Leon Boulevard
Coral Gables, Florida 33134 USA
P: 305.441.0440
F: 305.441.0198
E: aronfeld@aronfeld.com
       www.aronfeld.com

CPSIA information can be obtained
at www.ICGtesting.com
Printed in the USA
LVHW072158040121
675713LV00022B/296

* 9 7 8 1 4 5 2 0 7 5 1 5 0 *